Escape shuttle
Leia always thought the Resistance might have to leave D'Qar in a hurry. She has had shuttles prepared so the Resistance can escape.

BB-8
Poe's ever-loyal astromech droid joins him in his X-wing. BB-8 makes quick repairs as the ship takes damage, keeping Poe in the action.

POE DAMERON

Rose Tico
Rose is a technician in the Resistance fleet. She is tough and determined, but she has a sad past that she keeps hidden.

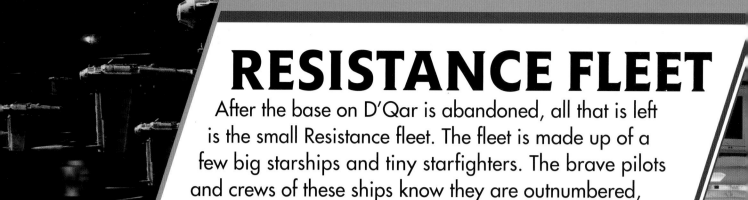

RESISTANCE FLEET

After the base on D'Qar is abandoned, all that is left is the small Resistance fleet. The fleet is made up of a few big starships and tiny starfighters. The brave pilots and crews of these ships know they are outnumbered, but they will fight to save the Resistance.

X-wing

X-wings are the Resistance's main starfighters. They are more powerful than First Order TIE fighters, but the Resistance doesn't have many of them.

Resistance cruiser

The most powerful ship in the fleet, the *Raddus,* is a Mon Calamari cruiser. It is General Leia's headquarters, and the main base for Resistance starfighter squadrons.

Tallie

Tallie is an A-wing interceptor pilot. Flying such a small, fast ship takes skill, instinct, and a lot of courage.

Medical frigate

The Resistance is small, and can't afford to lose people. The medical frigate treats wounded fighters so they can return to duty as quickly as possible.

A-wing

An updated starfighter design, the Resistance's A-wing interceptors are based on ships used by the old Rebel Alliance. Their huge twin engines make them lightning fast.

STAR WARS

THE LAST JEDI

ULTIMATE STICKER COLLECTION

HOW TO USE THIS BOOK

Read the captions, then find
the sticker that best fits the space.
(Hint: check the sticker labels for clues!)

•

There are lots of fantastic extra
stickers for creating your own
scenes throughout the book.

DK | Penguin
Random
House

Written and Edited by David Fentiman
Designer Chris Gould
Senior Designer Owen Bennett
Pre-production Producer Marc Staples
Senior Producer Mary Slater
Managing Editor Sadie Smith
Managing Art Editor Vicky Short
Publisher Julie Ferris
Art Director Lisa Lanzarini
Publishing Director Simon Beecroft

For Lucasfilm
Assistant Editor Samantha Holland
Art Director Troy Alders
Story Group James Waugh, Pablo Hidalgo,
Leland Chee, and Matt Martin
Image Unit Steve Newman, Newell Todd,
Gabrielle Levenson, Erik Sanchez, and Bryce Pinkos
Photographers Jonathan Olley, Ed Miller, John Wilson,
Shannon Kirbie, David James, and Bruno Dayan

First American Edition, 2017
Published in the United States by DK Publishing
345 Hudson Street, New York, New York 10014

Page design copyright © 2017 Dorling Kindersley Limited
DK, a Division of Penguin Random House LLC
17 18 19 20 21 10 9 8 7 6 5 4 3 2 1
001–298142–December/2017

© & TM 2017 LUCASFILM LTD.

All rights reserved.
Without limiting the rights under the copyright reserved above,
no part of this publication may be reproduced, stored in or introduced into a retrieval system,
or transmitted, in any form, or by any means (electronic, mechanical, photocopying,
recording, or otherwise), without the prior written permission of the copyright owner.

Published in Great Britain by Dorling Kindersley Limited.

A catalog record for this book is available from the Library of Congress.

ISBN: 978-1-4654-5556-7

DK books are available at special discounts when purchased in bulk for sales promotions,
premiums, fund-raising, or educational use. For details, contact:
DK Publishing Special Markets, 345 Hudson Street, New York, New York 10014
SpecialSales@dk.com

Printed and bound in China

A WORLD OF IDEAS:
SEE ALL THERE IS TO KNOW

www.dk.com
www.starwars.com

THE RESISTANCE

The brave Resistance has won a great victory, but it has not won the war. Although Starkiller Base has been destroyed, the evil First Order now knows where the Resistance is hiding. The Resistance must escape before the First Order arrives!

Planet D'Qar
The main Resistance base is on the planet D'Qar. Now that the First Order knows where it is, the Resistance has to leave quickly, before the base is destroyed.

Finn's recovery
Resistance fighter Finn was wounded during the Starkiller battle. A special suit full of healing bacta fluid will help him recover.

Poe Dameron
Poe is the best pilot in the Resistance, and proved himself during the battle at Starkiller Base. Although he is brave, Poe can sometimes be reckless.

General Leia
General Leia is legendary. She created the Resistance, and has led its fight against the First Order. Even during these desperate times, she won't give up hope of victory.

Kaydel Connix
Lieutenant Connix is one of the Resistance's smartest young officers. She admires Leia, and trusts that she will lead them all to safety.

Poe's X-wing

Poe has upgraded his X-wing with an extra booster. This will allow him to zoom in to attack the First Order fleet, and then escape again.

C'AI THRENALLI, X-WING PILOT

Poe's pilot gear

Just like other Resistance pilots, Poe wears survival gear when flying his X-wing. If his ship is damaged in battle, it will protect him.

Resistance BB unit

BB-8 is not the only BB unit in the Resistance. Other ball droids maintain ships and weapons, or fly into battle on board starfighters.

THE FIRST ORDER

Even though Starkiller Base has been destroyed, the First Order is still very powerful. It has a huge fleet of starships, and its crews and soldiers are highly trained. The First Order wants revenge, and to defeat the Resistance once and for all.

Stormtrooper
First Order stormtroopers are trained from a very young age. They follow orders without question, and work together in tight-knit squads.

General Hux
Ruthless General Hux destroyed the New Republic's capital world, Hosnian Prime. He has promised Snoke, the First Order's Supreme Leader, that he will hunt the Resistance down.

Executioner trooper
The First Order doesn't treat traitors kindly. These specialist troopers are tasked with eliminating dangerous or important prisoners.

Evil officer
First Order officers believe they should rule the galaxy, like the Empire once did. They will crush those who stand in their way.

Captain Phasma

Captain Phasma leads the First Order's stormtroopers. She was captured by Finn on Starkiller Base, but escaped. Now she wants revenge! In battle she wields a quicksilver baton.

EXECUTIONER TROOPER

Captain Peavey

Captain Peavey is an officer on Hux's Star Destroyer, *Finalizer*. He serves as Hux's second-in-command on board.

BB-9E

BB units do not just serve in the Resistance. The First Order uses them, too. First Order BB units are usually painted in dark colors.

BATTLE OF D'QAR

Just as the Resistance gets ready to leave D'Qar, the First Order fleet arrives! The Resistance starfighters and bombers will have to fight to hold them off. If the First Order destroys the Resistance cruiser, these brave fighters will be finished for good!

Resistance bomber

Bombers are powerful ships, but they are also slow. Each bomber carries a huge rack of proton bombs to drop on enemy targets.

Captain Canady

Canady is commander of the First Order dreadnought, *Fulminatrix*. He thinks he can smash the Resistance in a single battle.

TIE fighter

If the First Order's TIE fighters attack the bombers, the bombers won't stand a chance. Speedy A-wings and X-wings will have to shoot them down—fast.

Paige Tico

Fearless Paige is Rose's sister. She is a gunner on board a Resistance bomber. This is one of the most dangerous jobs in the fleet.

Proton bomb

Proton bombs are destructive weapons. They stick to the hull of a starship and then explode, ripping it open.

Dreadnought
Dreadnoughts are even bigger than regular Star Destroyers. Their huge cannons can blow up other warships in seconds.

PAIGE TICO

Bombardier Nix
Like all Resistance pilots, Nix knows that space combat is dangerous. Any battle could be his last, but he must fight to protect the galaxy.

LUKE'S ISLAND

Rey has traveled to the planet Ahch-To in search of the legendary Jedi Master, Luke Skywalker. Although she finds him, and the ruins of a Jedi temple, Rey does not get the welcome she expects. She also discovers that Luke's island holds many secrets.

Luke Skywalker
For years, Luke has lived the life of a simple hermit. His rough work clothes leave no clue that he was once a powerful Jedi Master.

Luke's hut
Luke lives in a stone hut that looks cold and uncomfortable. He keeps a few objects from his old life inside.

Caretaker
The caretakers are mysterious creatures. They live in a village on the island, and look after the crumbling Jedi ruins that dot the cliffs.

Porg
Porgs are birdlike creatures that nest on the island's slopes. They look really cute, and are also very smart.

Thala-siren
This huge creature doesn't look very appealing, but its milk is very good for you! Luke has learned to make use of whatever the island offers.

Luke´s compass

Luke once traveled the galaxy collecting ancient Jedi artifacts, such as this mysterious compass.

Chewbacca

With his friend Han gone, Chewbacca decides to help and protect Rey. While Rey learns the ways of the Jedi, Chewie stays close to the *Millennium Falcon*.

LUKE SKYWALKER

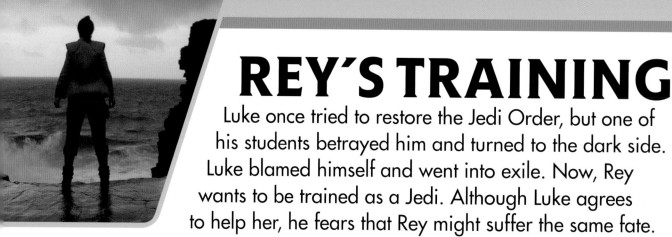

REY'S TRAINING

Luke once tried to restore the Jedi Order, but one of his students betrayed him and turned to the dark side. Luke blamed himself and went into exile. Now, Rey wants to be trained as a Jedi. Although Luke agrees to help her, he fears that Rey might suffer the same fate.

Luke's lightsaber
Perhaps the most famous lightsaber in the galaxy, this legendary weapon has belonged to Anakin Skywalker, Luke Skywalker, and now Rey.

The Jedi way
Everything that Rey knows about the Jedi comes from old stories. Luke shows her that the reality was very different.

Jedi temple
At the top of the highest mountain on the island is an ancient cavern. Outside, a rocky ledge overlooks the sea.

Old Master
When Luke puts on his old Jedi robes, he looks like the great Jedi Master he used to be.

REY

R2-D2
R2-D2 and Luke have been through many adventures together. Luke will always have a special place for R2 in his heart.

Island explorer
Luke's island has many mysteries. Rey explores the ancient ruins and hidden caves, looking for lost Jedi secrets.

Millennium Falcon
After Han Solo lost his life during the battle on Starkiller Base, Rey took over as pilot of the *Millennium Falcon*.

CANTO BIGHT

Together, Finn and Rose realize that there is a way to save the Resistance Fleet—they must travel to Canto Bight and find a master codebreaker. Canto Bight is famous for its casinos and entertainments, but hidden behind all of the luxury, there is a darker side to this city.

Finn and Rose
When they first meet, Rose thinks Finn is a coward who is trying to run away from the Resistance. Later, she realizes that together they make a great team.

Cantonica
The planet Cantonica is mostly barren desert, but there is a single clear, blue sea. Canto Bight city lies on its shore.

Resistance light shuttle
Although Poe agrees with Finn and Rose's plan, the other Resistance leaders don't know about it. Finn and Rose have to leave the fleet in secret, in a stolen shuttle.

The casino
The big attraction on Canto Bight is the gaming halls. Inside these luxurious buildings, vast fortunes can be won or lost.

Canto Bight police
With so many wealthy people in town, and so much money on show, the Canto Bight police will instantly arrest anyone who looks suspicious.

Canto Bight speeder

Those who come to Canto Bight want to show off their riches. The streets are full of expensive speeders, built out of exotic materials in unusual designs.

Rose's medallion

Rose's medallion is almost identical to her sister Paige's. It is made from a rare metal known as Haysian smelt.

ROSE TICO

THE CASINO

Located on the planet Cantonica, the city of Canto Bight is unlike anywhere else in the galaxy. It is glitzy, glamorous, and very, very wealthy. For Finn and Rose, used to the shabby Resistance fleet, the Canto Bight casino is a strange and exciting place.

Casino guest

The richest aliens in the galaxy come to Canto Bight to have fun. All kinds of species are here, and all of them wear the most expensive clothes imaginable.

Gaming machine

There are lots of different games to play in the casino hall. These round gaming machines look a lot like BB-8!

Rich villain

Many who come to Canto Bight have made their fortunes in very unpleasant ways.

Casino tokens

The casino guests use these brightly colored tokens to play the games in the casino.

CASINO GUESTS

Waiter droid

The waiters in the casino are advanced protocol droids. They are programmed to look after the guests and keep them happy.

Party girl

Canto Bight attracts lots of shady characters. This guest looks innocent, but sometimes beauty can hide great evil.

Barman

Serving drinks to aliens from every sector of space, with very different tastes, takes a lot of skill.

ESCAPE!

Just when they find the master codebreaker, Finn and Rose get arrested by the Canto Bight police and thrown into jail! Things don't look good—if they can't find a way to escape from Canto Bight, the Resistance fleet will be destroyed!

DJ

DJ is a mysterious figure. Finn and Rose don't even know his real name. DJ stands for "don't join," which is his attitude to life. He is a thief and a criminal, but DJ claims he can help them.

DJ´s ship

Just when Finn and Rose seem trapped, DJ rescues them in his ship. It is fast and expensive-looking, and Finn and Rose realize that DJ must have stolen it.

Rose´s ring

Rose wears a ring with a Resistance symbol hidden inside. If she shows it to people who support the Resistance, they will help her.

Canto Bight jail

For some, Canto Bight is not what they imagined. Those who make trouble or run out of money usually end up in the city jail.

Canto Bight police speeder

The Canto Bight police use these flashy-looking speeders to chase after fleeing suspects.

Fathier

Fathier racing is a Canto Bight specialty. The huge, graceful fathiers are prized for their speed and agility, and the races always draw big crowds.

Fathier jockey

It takes nerves of steel to climb onto the back of a fathier. These jockeys need super-fast reflexes to avoid falling off!

Stable keeper

The fathier stable keeper is a fearsome creature. He is mean both to the fathiers, and the poor stable children who care for them.

FINN

Use the
extra stickers
to create your
own scene.

IN COMMAND

It takes a lot of bravery to be a leader. When there is trouble or danger, soldiers look to their commanders to make hard decisions. The leaders of the Resistance know that everyone is relying on them. If they fail, then the galaxy is doomed.

Leia's homing beacon
Leia wears a beacon on her arm. This device will allow Rey to find the Resistance fleet wherever it is in the galaxy, so she can return once her training is complete.

Wounded leader
With General Leia in command, the Resistance fleet escapes from the First Order at D'Qar. Unfortunately Leia is injured during the battle, and others must then step up to lead.

Bridge guard
Guards are stationed by the doors to the cruiser's bridge. With First Order spies everywhere, the commanders can't take any chances.

Cruiser bridge
The bridge of the *Raddus* is a hive of activity. From here, courses are plotted, strategies are planned, and important decisions are made.

Commander D'acy
One of the senior officers on the cruiser, D'acy is in charge of the bridge crew. She serves Leia and Vice Admiral Holdo.

Admiral Ackbar

One of Leia's most trusted officers, Admiral Ackbar has commanded starships for decades. This battle, though, is tougher than anything he has faced before.

C-3PO

C-3PO is Leia's personal assistant, and they have been friends for a very long time. When Leia is wounded, C-3PO takes care of her, waiting by her bedside.

Vice Admiral Holdo

Vice Admiral Amilyn Holdo is an old friend of Leia's. After Leia is hurt, Holdo takes command of the fleet. She is an experienced officer, but Poe does not trust her.

KYLO REN

Kylo Ren, the First Order's greatest warrior, is actually General Leia's son. Supreme Leader Snoke turned him to the dark side of the Force. He fought Rey on Starkiller Base—although she defeated him, Kylo's anger just makes him stronger.

Dark disciple

Kylo Ren is Supreme Leader Snoke's powerful apprentice. Snoke senses the conflict inside Kylo, and uses it to grow Kylo's powers.

Kylo's shuttle

When not piloting his TIE silencer, Kylo uses this bat-winged shuttle to get around.

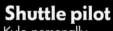

Kylo's lightsaber

Built by Kylo himself, this unusual lightsaber has three blades. In Kylo's hands, it is a devastating weapon.

Shuttle pilot

Kylo personally chooses those who serve under him. It is an honor for any First Order crew member, but Kylo's temper also makes it a dangerous job.

Jedi destroyer

Years ago, Kylo turned against the other Jedi apprentices training with Luke Skywalker, and destroyed them all.

KYLO
REN

First Order medical droid
Kylo was wounded during his duel with Rey. A medical droid heals his injuries.

Kylo's mask
Darth Vader, a Sith Lord in the Galactic Empire, was Kylo Ren's grandfather. Kylo honors Vader by wearing a mask, just like his grandfather did.

TIE silencer
Kylo Ren's personal starfighter is a new TIE fighter design. It combines the heavy weapons of a bomber with the speed and agility of a fighter.

THE *SUPREMACY*

The dark heart of the First Order is the *Supremacy*. This huge ship is Supreme Leader Snoke's mobile headquarters. It is heavily armed and almost impossible to destroy. Inside, Snoke commands the First Order from his throne room.

Snoke

Snoke is the First Order's shadowy supreme leader. He is cruel, ruthless, extremely smart, and very powerful with the dark side of the Force.

Mega-Destroyer

The *Supremacy* is the First Order's flagship. If it can get close enough, this powerful vessel will easily destroy the entire Resistance fleet.

Praetorian Guard

Snoke's bodyguards wear red suits of armor and carry fearsome weapons. They are some of the most skilled warriors in the First Order.

Praetorian weapons

The Praetorians' weapons are unique, just like their armor. They are designed to combine in several different ways.

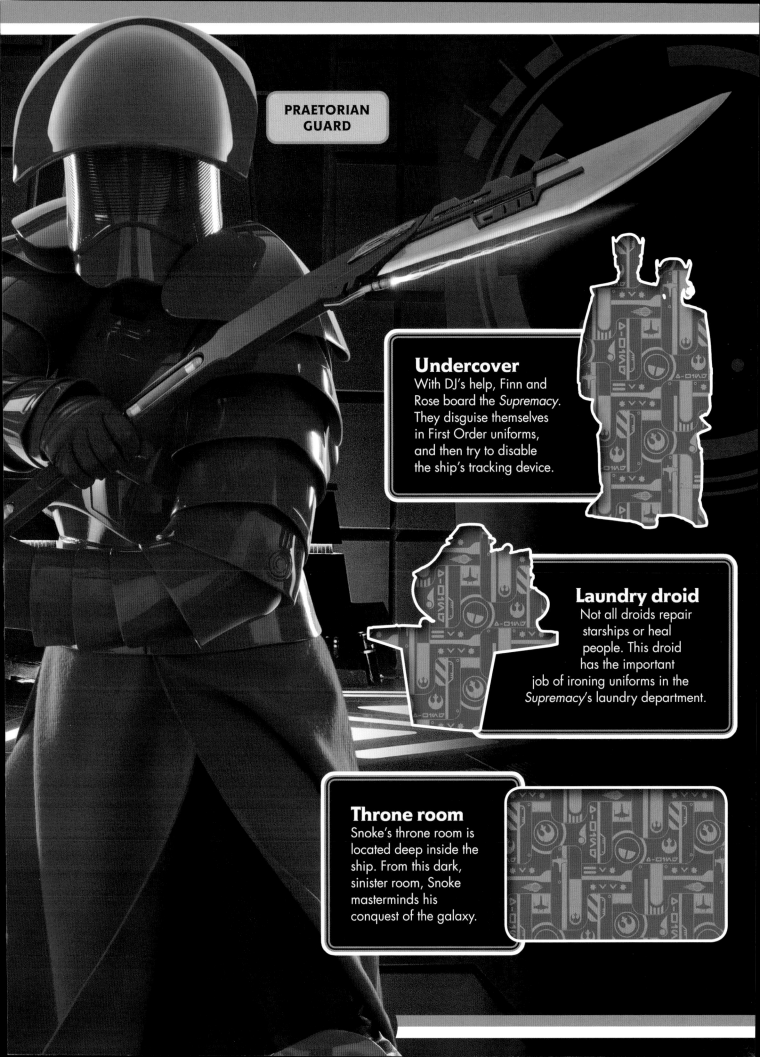

PRAETORIAN
GUARD

Undercover
With DJ's help, Finn and
Rose board the *Supremacy*.
They disguise themselves
in First Order uniforms,
and then try to disable
the ship's tracking device.

Laundry droid
Not all droids repair
starships or heal
people. This droid
has the important
job of ironing uniforms in the
Supremacy's laundry department.

Throne room
Snoke's throne room is
located deep inside the
ship. From this dark,
sinister room, Snoke
masterminds his
conquest of the galaxy.

INVASION FORCE

The First Order has more than just fleets of starships. When it decides to invade a planet, it also has a huge arsenal of ground vehicles to choose from. Just like in the Galactic Empire, giant armored walkers are used to smash through enemy armies.

AT-M6
AT-M6s are among the most powerful weapons in the First Order army. These gigantic machines tower above even AT-ATs. Each carries a huge cannon, and their fists can smash through the toughest armor.

Gunner
These skilled technicians crew the First Order's heavy weapons. They have devastating firepower at their fingertips.

AT-ST
The AT-ST is based on an old Imperial design. This two-legged walker can move fast over rough terrain.

Superlaser siege cannon
Some defenses are too tough for normal weapons. When needed, the First Order uses massive mobile superlaser cannons to blast enemy positions apart.

Siege cannon tug
The siege cannon is so big that it has to be dragged into position. Special walkers pull it along using strong cables.

AT–AT
AT-ATs were originally used by the Imperial army. The First Order has upgraded them, making them even more deadly.

BATTLE OF CRAIT

With nowhere left to run, the Resistance lands on a small planet named Crait. It must make its final stand here. Crait is a strange world—the surface is covered by a thin white crust of salt, with bright-red minerals hidden underneath.

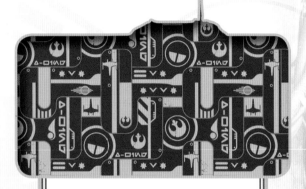

Vulptex

These unusual creatures live in the dark tunnels of the old rebel base. Their crystal bodies make a strange tinkling noise when they run.

Abandoned base

Crait was the site of a rebel base during the war against the Empire. Many years later, the abandoned base is still there.

Leading the charge

Faced with overwhelming odds, Poe leads the few remaining Resistance pilots into battle.

Resistance trooper

Many Resistance fighters have not made it this far. The survivors prepare to defend the base for as long as they can.

Ski speeder

The Resistance finds these ancient-looking speeders in the abandoned rebel base. They don't look like they have been used in years, but the Resistance has few options left.

General
Ematt

Resistance medic
The Resistance's medics bravely try to save lives while the battle rages all around them.

Fearless Finn
Finn joins Poe in the ski speeder attack on the First Order army. He will fight to defend the Resistance, whatever happens.

Crait landscape
The Crait landscape is barren. Flat deserts stretch to the horizon, broken by sharp ridges and deep canyons.

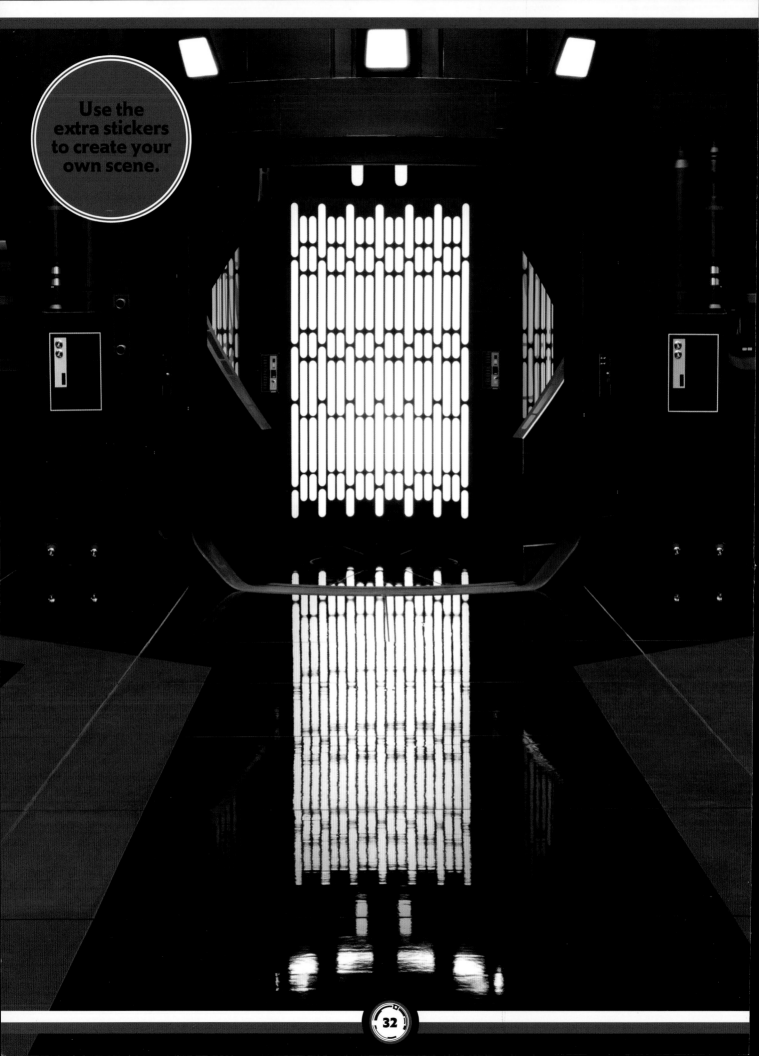

Use the extra stickers to create your own scene.